The BREATHING TREES

by Mark Weakland
illustrated by Chris Jevons

a Capstone company — publishers for children

Engage Literacy is published in the UK by Raintree.
Raintree is an imprint of Capstone Global Library Limited, a company incorporated in England and Wales having its registered office at 264 Banbury Road, Oxford, OX2 7DY – Registered company number: 6695582

www.raintree.co.uk

Editorial credits
Jill Kalz, editor; Richard Parker, designer; Katy LaVigne, production specialist

21 20 19 18
10 9 8 7 6 5 4 3 2 1
Printed and bound in India.

The Breathing Trees

ISBN: 978 1 4747 4702 8

Contents

Chapter 1:

Trees in space

"Hello, you little things," said Nova. "Wow, you have grown!"

"Thank you," said Jarrell, who had just appeared in the doorway. "But I'm not growing much."

Next to him, Gemm, tall for her age, grinned. "I am! I didn't think anyone could tell!"

Nova turned to her friends, a slight frown on her face. "I wasn't talking to you. I was talking to the trees."

Jarrell and Gemm peered over Nova's shoulder. They could see a metal box containing a set of five saplings. The box of young trees sat in front of a round window. Outside the window, black space and countless sparkling stars spread in every direction.

Nova, Gemm and Jarrell were travelling with their parents to Earth Colony Five. A giant space station, it circled around the planet Jupiter. The journey from Earth to Jupiter was a long one, more than two years. But the children were never bored. On the ship there was a cinema, two gyms and a canteen where people often gathered. Each of the friends had jobs aboard the ship. And there were many school projects to complete.

Gemm looked down at the saplings. "So, how are our little gas-makers? Are they making more oxygen?"

"No, not really," said Nova. "So far they're making the same amount as on Earth. I was hoping they'd make more."

"Yes, me, too," said Jarrell. "Our idea was that trees increase their oxygen output in space. If these saplings don't start making more oxygen, Mr Nubbins is going to say, 'I told you so!'"

Mr Nubbins was their teacher on Earth. Every other week the three sent him a report describing how their school projects were coming along.

Nova frowned. "Yep, that's exactly what he would say. Good old 'I Told You So' Nubbins."

Jarrell was frowning, too. "It's not like we can make up the results. We have to report what we see."

"I know what my mum would say," said Gemm, leaping onto a nearby chair and pointing a finger at her friends. "She'd say, 'Brains are for changing, not complaining.'"

"What does that mean?" asked Jarrell.

Gemm jumped down and picked up the plants. By the look on her face, Nova and Jarrell could tell that a crazy thought was forming in her mind. "If we don't like the end result, we should make a change. You know, try something different. I have an idea."

Chapter 2:
The Loft

"Oh dear," said Jarrell. "Why am I suddenly worried?"

"Don't worry," said Gemm, grinning. "I won't get us into too much trouble."

"Hey!" said Nova. "I know what you're thinking. The Loft!"

Jarrell looked worried. "What? We can't take our trees to the Loft. They'll float away. And we're not supposed to go in there without an adult."

The Loft was what the children called the cargo bay at the very tip of the ship. It was a large space used for storing all kinds of things, from food to equipment. The room was not attached to the rest of the ship. This meant it did not rotate. Rather, it sat still at the end of a short tunnel. Because it didn't rotate, the storage room had very little gravity. This microgravity meant that anything not strapped down floated.

"I was in there once," said Nova. "By myself. Dad and I took some cargo there. I dropped my pocket vid but didn't know it. Dad sent me back in to get it." She reached over her shoulder and gave herself a pat on the back. "I did pretty well in microgravity. Floating is fun!"

"Yes, but not for tiny trees," said Jarrell.

"We'll glue the bottom of the plant pots to the container," said Gemm. "Then we'll strap the container down."

"How will we water them?" asked Jarrell. "Water floats in microgravity."

Gemm scratched her head. "Hmm. Let me think." She turned and looked out of the window.

"I've got it!" shouted Nova.

Jarrell and Gemm jumped. "Gosh," said Jarrell. "How excited are you?"

Nova ignored him. "We can wind the drip hoses through the bottom of the pots and cover them with soil. The water will soak into the soil from below. It won't have a chance to float away."

"Good idea," said Gemm, giving her a high five and almost dropping the tree saplings.

Jarrell was still thinking. "But it's more than the microgravity that I'm worried about. The cargo bay is the part of the ship most likely to get struck by flying space rocks. Or hit with high-energy radiation waves zooming through space."

"We'll work fast," said Gemm.

"Yes," said Nova. "It won't take long." She put her arm around Gemm's shoulders. "We'll use teamwork. One of us of will check on the trees every week. We'll share the job."

"What will I tell my parents I'm doing?" asked Jarrell.

"Don't tell them anything," said Gemm, heading towards the cabin door. It slid open by itself as Gemm approached, and she stepped through. Nova followed closely behind.

Jarrell frowned. "My mum says leaving out part of the truth is still a lie."

But Gemm hadn't heard him. Neither had Nova. They were already skipping down the ship's corridor, the container of saplings bouncing between them.

Chapter 3:
Floating Friends

The three friends grabbed a bottle of super glue, a spool of drip hose and three straps from the supply room. Then they headed towards the end of the ship. Soon they came to the tunnel that led to the cargo bay. A sign on the wall said *Caution: Microgravity Area*.

Gemm didn't slow down. She stepped up to the door and swiped her key card. With a quiet swish, the door slid open. Ahead, the tunnel stretched into the distance. Soft lights lit the way.

Jarrell stepped inside and looked around. "What are the grooves on the floor and ceiling for?"

"They're rungs," said Nova. "For pulling yourself along with your hands. The further in you walk, the less gravity there is. About halfway in, you'll find it very difficult to keep your feet on the floor. Three-quarters of the way in, you'll start floating."

"Come on, let's go!" said Gemm.

"Wait," said Nova. "We have to get the trees ready."

The friends carefully took the trees out of the pots. Next, they threaded the drip hose through. Then they replanted the saplings.

Finally, they squeezed a line of super glue around the bottom of the pots. They put the pots in the container and waited for the glue to dry.

As soon as the glue had dried, they walked down the tunnel. Jarrell and Nova carried the container between them. By the end, all three were floating. The container was floating, too.

At first it was hard to get around in the cargo bay. The friends had to push off with their feet and then use their arms and hands to guide themselves. But the longer they floated, the easier it was to move from one place to the next. Soon Jarrell was pushing off the wall and doing slow cartwheels through the air. "This is amazing!" he shouted.

"Come on, Jarrell," said Gemm. "We have work to do."

In the end they didn't need the straps. They just wedged the box of saplings between two large containers. Nearby there was a service light.

"OK," said Gemm. "They won't float away. They have a light source. Now all they need is water."

"One drink of water, coming up!" said Nova, bending down.

Nova put the narrow end of a large bulb into the container's tube. Then she squeezed the bulb. Water ran into and through the tube. They could see the soil in each container get darker as the water soaked in.

"It's working!" said Nova.

"Now all we have to do is take an oxygen reading," said Gemm. She pressed a button on the side of the container. Red numbers and letters appeared.

"Five millilitres an hour," said Gemm. "Record that, Jarrell."

Jarrell pressed a button on his pocket vid. "Got it."

"OK," said Nova. "We've finished for today." She pushed off and floated towards the tunnel opening. "Gemm, you can take the first week. Come in once a day and take an oxygen reading."

"Aye, aye, captain," said Gemm. She pushed off a container and zoomed through the air. "Wahoo! I'm a shooting star. Look at me, I'm – oof! Ouch!"

"More like a big lump of space rock," said Nova as she watched Gemm overshoot the tunnel entrance and crash into the wall. "Be careful."

"Yes!" said Jarrell. "We may not have weight in here, but we're still made up of matter. We still have mass. Crashes hurt, even in microgravity."

Chapter 4:
Locked in

For weeks the friends took turns checking the oxygen made by the plants. One day Gemm and Nova were sitting in the ship's canteen. Suddenly Jarrell burst in.

"Seven millilitres an hour!" he shouted.

"Whff?" said Nova through a mouthful of salad.

"Seven millilitres an hour," repeated Jarrell. "The saplings are making seven millilitres of oxygen an hour. The rate is rising!"

"That's great!" said Gemm. "I can't wait to tell Mr Nubbins. Now we can be the ones saying, 'I told you so.'"

"I think we should watch for one more week," said Nova.

"Agreed," said Jarrell. "I'll finish this week. You do next week, Gemm."

At the end of the sixth week, Gemm reported that the saplings were making eight millilitres of oxygen an hour. The friends were so excited that they all wanted to see the readout. Into the tunnel they went, running and bouncing off each other as they floated into the cargo bay.

"Wow," said Nova, admiring the saplings. "They're growing into real trees."

Gemm floated upside down in the air above them. She pulled herself closer. "Yes, just look at their–"

CRACK!

The sound was as loud as a firecracker.

Jarrell looked around in a panic. "What was that?" he asked.

"I don't know," said Nova, her eyes wide. "It sounded like something breaking."

From somewhere high above came a HISSS! It sounded like air rushing through a hole. Then WHOOP! WHOOP! WHOOP! WHOOP! It was the alarm horn. Red lights along the walls began to flash. Quick as a wink, the door to the tunnel slid shut.

"The emergency system's on!" screamed Gemm. "We've been hit by a space rock!"

Nova gave a push with her legs. She flew across the room towards the tunnel door. Grabbing a handle by the door, she hit the "open" button with her thumb. Nothing happened. She hit the button again and again. The alarm horn blared. The lights flashed. The door stayed shut.

Gemm turned to Jarrell. "The air's leaking out," she said. "And we're locked in!"

Chapter 5:

Time for teamwork

"What shall we do?" cried Jarrell. His eyes were as big as dinner plates.

Gemm took a deep breath. "OK, first of all, don't panic. Second, think about our disaster training."

Every person aboard every spaceship that sailed from Earth had many, many hours of disaster training. Even young children were trained on what to do if their ship lost gravity or if something hit it.

"Right," said Jarrell, calming down. "Let's see if we can find the communication panel. We can use it to call the control room and get help."

Nova was still next to the tunnel. She was no longer pressing the button. She was looking around carefully. When Gemm and Jarrell joined her, she said, "There should be a panel here. But I can't find it."

"That's what we thought, too. I bet it's behind those," said Jarrell. He pointed to the containers that lined either side of the doorway. "Come on, help me move them."

WHOOP! WHOOP! WHOOP! WHOOP! The alarm horn seemed louder than before. Jarrell pushed against the stack of containers on the right side of the door. Every time he pushed, he shot backwards.

Jarrell turned to his friends. "I need something to push against. I can't create forward motion without pushing backwards on something."

"Time for teamwork," said Gemm. "I have an idea!"

"Well, share it, Einstein," said Nova. "We've got an emergency here!"

Gemm pointed to the containers on the left side of the door. "I'll brace my feet against those boxes. Nova, you float up and put your feet on my shoulders. Then Jarrell, you float up and put your feet on Nova's shoulders. When Jarrell's arms push against the stack, his legs will push against us. He won't shoot backwards."

Nova and Gemm floated into position. They formed a line of solid bone and muscle. Jarrell leaped and floated to the top. Nova grabbed his feet and held them against her shoulders. "On the count of three, push. One … two … three!"

Nova and Gemm braced themselves as Jarrell pushed. Gemm saw the containers shift. "One more time!" she shouted. "One … two … three!"

Jarrell threw himself against the containers. His legs pushed down on Nova and Gemm as his arms pushed up. The stack wobbled and then fell.

The communication panel was a metre off the ground. Gemm lunged forwards, causing Nova and Jarrell to spin out and then float away. She entered the code for the ship's control room and hit the talk button.

"Control!" she shouted. "Control! This is Gemm, Nova and Jarrell. We're trapped in the cargo bay. The air is leaking out. Please open the door to the tunnel straight away!"

A deep voice came from the panel. "Gemm, this is Captain Conway. Don't panic. Step back from the door."

Gemm stepped back just as Nova and Jarrell floated down to join her. The captain's voice sounded from the panel again. "I can't hold the door open for very long. I am going to count to five. On one, I will open the door. On counts two, three and four, you must get into the tunnel. On five, I'm going to close the door. Do you understand?"

"We understand!" the children said.

"One …" said the captain. The door slid open. "Two …" The children raced for the door and began pulling themselves inside the tunnel. "Three … four …"

"We're in!" cried Gemm.

"Five!" The door slid shut. On the other side, the three friends breathed a sigh of relief.

Chapter 6:

Trees on Earth

For being in the cargo bay without permission, the three friends were not allowed to spend time together for a week. Nor were they allowed to go to the canteen, use the gym or talk on their pocket vids. The only things they could do were their homework and their space jobs.

Nova was allowed to go and bring out the saplings. This time her dad went with her. But she had to wait until the week was over before she could tell her friends the good news. The saplings were safe. And they were still making a lot of oxygen.

Two weeks later, Gemm and Nova were back in the canteen. Jarrell ran up to their table. "Guess what?" he said, out of breath.

"Whff?" said Nova through a mouthful of cheese and crackers.

"You know how I sent our results to Mr Nubbins last week?" Jarrell said.

"You mean the results of our tree experiment?" Gemm asked. "How the saplings were making more oxygen?"

Jarrell's eyes gleamed. "Yes!"

"What about it?" asked Nova.

"I've just heard back from him," Jarrell said.

"And?" said Nova and Gemm together.

Jarrell smiled. "He gave our results to some scientists. They all got very excited. And now they're going to grow hundreds of saplings in the microgravity area of Earth Colony One! Because of us!"

"The moon colony?" said Nova.

"Yep," said Jarrell. "Then they're going to ship the trees back to Earth and plant them. The scientists think the trees will take in more carbon dioxide and give out more oxygen. The trees will help clean Earth's air! Isn't that exciting?"

Gemm grinned. "Almost as exciting as being trapped in a cargo bay."